MW00954825

The Pocket Book

The Pocket Book

by Josephine Haskell Aldridge

illustrated by René King Moreno

SIMON & SCHUSTER BOOKS FOR YOUNG READERS
Published by Simon & Schuster
New York London Toronto Sydney Tokyo Singapore

SIMON & SCHUSTER BOOKS FOR YOUNG READERS
Simon & Schuster Building, Rockefeller Center
1230 Avenue of the Americas, New York, New York 10020
Text copyright © 1994 by Josephine Haskell Aldridge
Illustrations copyright © 1994 by René King Moreno
SIMON & SCHUSTER BOOKS FOR YOUNG READERS
is a trademark of Simon & Schuster.
The text for this book is set in 16 point Maximus.
The illustrations were done in pastel.
Manufactured in the United States of America.

10 9 8 7 6 5 4 3 2 1

Library of Congress Cataloging-in-Publication Data
Aldridge, Josephine Haskell. The pocket book/by
Josephine Haskell Aldridge; illustrated by René King
Moreno. Summary: At the pocket store, Abby has
trouble deciding what kind of pocket she wants for
her new dress. [1. Pockets—Fiction. 2. Clothing
and dress—Fiction. 3. Stories in rhyme.]
I. Moreno, René King, ill. II. Title.
PZ8.3.A368Po 1993 [E]—dc20 CIP 93-1699
ISBN: 0-671-87128-5

Abby had a new dress;
but it didn't have a pocket,
so she walked with Mommy
to the pocket store.
She wanted a pocket,
a truly blue pocket,
like the square smock pocket
she had before.

A kangaroo was there first.
She wanted one, too—
the size of a baby
kangaroo.

A pelican stood
on one leg and said
he needed a pocket
under his head.

The pocket man was busy
sewing pockets on
a friend,
so Abby looked at pockets
from beginning to end.

She found one truly blue
and a truly red one, too;
a short size, a tall size,
and one to match her big blue eyes;

a round one, a triangle,
and a tickly fur tangle;
a sort of striped dandy
(like peppermint candy)
and a buttoned navy blue.
Which one would do?

Abby tried to decide,
and tried, and then
decided that
she needed ten.

Mommy said ten
pockets were too
many:

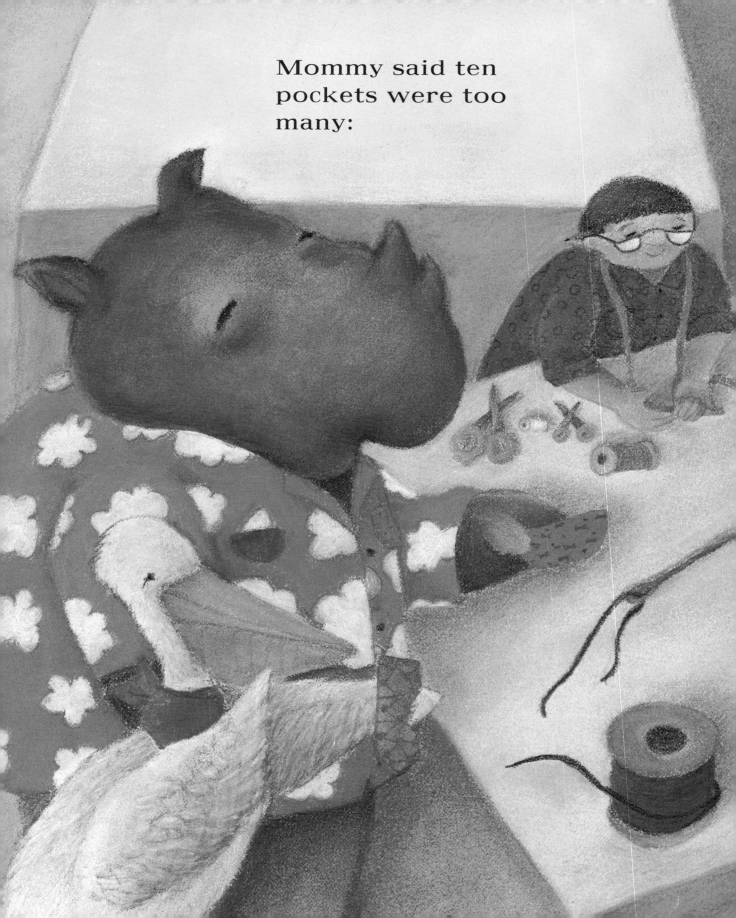

Abby could have
one, or she
couldn't have
any.

Abby told Mommy
that she could really use ten:

1 for her pencil

and 2 for her pen,

3 for a little bear
with a little bear name,

4 for a daisy chain
(when daisy days came),

5 for a furry brown
caterpillar round,

6 for the lucky pink
pebble on the ground,

7 for her crayons,

8 for her comb,

9 for a seashell
she wants to take home,

10 for a book
for a rainy day.

So Mommy said yes,
and the man said
okay.

And do you know,
or would you guess,

where he sewed
all ten pockets
on Abby's new dress?